The Christmas Dolls

The Christmas Dolls

A Butterfield Square Story

by Carol Beach York

illustrated by Victoria de Larrea

A Yearling Book

For my husband Dick,
with love

Published by
Dell Publishing Co., Inc.
1 Dag Hammarskjold Plaza
New York, New York 10017
Copyright © 1967 by Carol Beach York
All rights reserved. For information contact Franklin Watts, Inc.,
New York, New York 10019.
Yearling ® TM 913705, Dell Publishing Co., Inc.
Reprinted by arrangement with Franklin Watts, Inc.
ISBN: 0-440-41254-4
Printed in the United States of America
First Yearling printing—November 1976
Second Dell Printing—October 1977

Contents

1

The Christmas Dolls

It was two days before Christmas. A chill December wind swept along the pavement and around the corners of Butterfield Square. All the old brick houses stood in a row, stiff and straight. Through the black iron fences blew the wind; across the frozen ground; hard against the doors with their polished knockers and heavy doorknobs; hard against the windows with their little square panes.

Above the gate at Number 18, the sign that said *The Good Day Orphanage for Girls* creaked in the wind. Inside, in the parlor, a fire burned on the hearth.

In the parlor, Miss Lavender and Miss Plum were unpacking the Christmas toys that had been sent from the clock factory across town. Every year at Christmastime the people who worked at the clock factory brought used toys to work and fixed them up as good as new and sent them around to places where plenty of Christmas toys were needed. Every year they sent a big box to Number 18 Butterfield Square.

Miss Lavender and Miss Plum had decided to light a fire in the fireplace because it was so close to Christmas, and it just seemed that they were in the spirit to have a fire. They had a good furnace in the basement to heat the house, and the fire was only to make the room more cheerful and cozy. It was not a great hearty fire, for Miss Lavender and Miss Plum were careful not to use too much wood, but it gave a bright glow around the hearth and it did make the whole parlor more cheerful.

This year, the Christmas toys sent to The Good Day were all dolls, one for every girl, and when Florabelle was taken out of the big brown cardboard box the first thing she saw was the tiny fire sparkling behind the grate. Florabelle's eyes were clear green glass, and the fire reflected in them made them shine.

"Oh, this one's only a rag doll," Miss Plum said, looking at Florabelle with disappointment.

"Oh, dear, so it is." Miss Lavender looked up over the top of her round gold-rimmed spectacles. Her face was flushed very warm and pink from bending over to take the dolls out of the big cardboard box. She was much shorter than Miss Plum and was round and plump, with her soft white hair heaped up in curls on her head. Miss Plum was thin and stood very straight, as though she had a ruler against her back. Her gray hair was tied up tight in a bun; no one had ever seen it any other way.

Miss Lavender and Miss Plum looked at Florabelle uncertainly. All the other dolls had smooth hard pink heads and arms and legs. Some had eyes that opened and closed, and some had hair that could be combed. But Florabelle was rather flat and limp, with yellow yarn braids and sewed-on glass eyes and a mouth made of red darning thread.

"Well, anyway," Miss Plum said at last, "her dress is pretty."

"But she has no shoes," Miss Lavender said. However, just then Miss Plum's attention was caught by the next doll she saw lying in the cardboard box, and she set Florabelle down without another thought.

"Look at this, Miss Lavender," Miss Plum exclaimed, and she took a small doll in a blue dress out of the box. Poor Florabelle, who had felt very embarrassed to be stared at and talked about so, forgot herself entirely when she saw the doll that Miss Plum was now holding. The doll's face was very pretty, with eyes that opened and closed and a smiling mouth with tiny white teeth showing—but her head had been put on backward! Nor was this even the worst of it—she had lost her hair and her smooth doll head gleamed baldly, like a pink Easter egg.

"Oh, *dear!*" Miss Lavender did not know what to say at all when she saw this.

"This doll was put in the box by mistake, it's plain to see," Miss Plum decided. "She was over-looked when the toys were repaired."

"I guess *so,*" Miss Lavender agreed.

"Just look," Miss Plum said. "Head on back-ward. Wig gone."

"And *she* has no shoes, either," Miss Lavender murmured. Florabelle looked at the other dolls lying along the window seat. They all had shoes, and some of them had stockings, too.

"Well, let's just set her aside for now," Miss Plum suggested. "Maybe we can fix her ourselves."

"Yes," said Miss Lavender, who always agreed with what Miss Plum said, "maybe we can."

Florabelle watched as Miss Plum set the bald-headed doll on the top of a bookcase nearby. Miss Plum put the doll down with her face toward the wall, and the smooth pink back of her head turned out to the room. Oh, she can't see a thing, poor dear, Florabelle thought to herself sympa-thetically, but there was nothing she could do to help—and she was not so very happy about her own affairs either. One by one as the other dolls were taken out of the box it became clear to see that Florabelle was the only rag doll; the only doll with glass-button eyes and a thread mouth; the only doll (except the poor doll on the bookcase) without shoes.

In the corner of the room, a Christmas tree stood ready to be trimmed, and on the floor beside the tree a box of ornaments was open and several long loops of silver tinsel spilled out over the carpet. On a sofa before the fireplace, a pile of angel costumes made of thin white gauzy material covered the cushions and almost hid the sewing basket from sight. A clock on the mantel above the fireplace ticked quickly along toward three o'clock—and several times Miss Plum looked at it anxiously. "We must have the dolls wrapped by three fifteen," she would remind Miss Lavender, "because the girls are coming then to try on the costumes."

"Yes, we must hurry," Miss Lavender would agree, whenever Miss Plum reminded her about the time.

One by one they put each Christmas doll in a layer of white tissue paper and then a layer of pretty red and green Christmas paper, and then tied up the package securely with red ribbon which they pulled from a large spool on the table by the window seat. The dolls talked among themselves as they waited to be wrapped up, which was all right, of course, for Miss Plum and Miss Lavender weren't able to hear dolls talk. The dolls were all so happy to be fixed up as good as new again and to be going to belong to little girls who would play with them and love them.

"I've been up in an attic for three years," one doll said, sighing with delight. "It's wonderful to see something besides storage boxes and cobwebs again. Look at the Christmas tree! Look at the snow!"

"Yes, yes, see the snow!" all the other dolls clamored happily.

Indeed, beyond the window a light snow had begun to fall as the afternoon passed along; across Butterfield Square it whirled in the wind. When Miss Lavender noticed the snow she said, "Look,

Miss Plum. Our snow has come in time for Christmas, after all."

Miss Plum looked out at the snow silently, and then she said, "I think that calls for another log, don't you, Miss Lavender?"

"Oh, yes, indeed I do," Miss Lavender said, and scurried across the room to the fireplace and put another piece of wood into the fire. How brightly and warmly the fire flared up, crackling and dancing. "Isn't it lovely, Miss Plum?"

Miss Plum watched the fire a moment, nodding with satisfaction, and then she said, "And just look at the clock, Miss Lavender. We must be done by three fifteen."

So on they went, wrapping the dolls in a layer of tissue paper and then a layer of Christmas paper, tying them up tightly with the red ribbon.

"I've got a new dress and bonnet," one of the dolls said.

"They gave me new hair," another said.

One after the other they were wrapped up and hidden from sight for the time being inside the paper and ribbon.

The dolls were nearly all wrapped, when suddenly Miss Plum—who had been silently counting to herself how many dolls were yet to be wrapped—dropped the tissue paper she was holding and said, "Wait a minute, Miss Lavender—they've sent too many."

"Oh?" Miss Lavender was in the middle of tying a bow with the red ribbon, and she looked up doubtfully, holding her finger in the bow.

Miss Plum was counting out loud this time to be sure there would be no mistake. "—twenty-five—twenty-six—twenty-seven—twenty-eight—twenty-*nine!* Just as I thought. There's one extra."

"Oh, dear," Miss Lavender said. "Twenty-*nine?* You're right, Miss Plum. One extra. In fact," she added with dismay, "two extra." She nodded over to the bookcase where the bald doll sat staring into the wall.

Miss Plum looked at the dolls and tried to decide what to do. At last she said, "Let's just set aside this rag doll. It's the only rag one."

"All right," Miss Lavender agreed. She smiled kindly at Florabelle over the top of her gold-rimmed glasses as Miss Plum placed Florabelle on top of the bookcase.

But Florabelle was not very much comforted by Miss Lavender's smile. From the bookcase she watched unhappily while the rest of the dolls were wrapped. On Christmas morning they would be unwrapped again by laughing little girls who would hug them and kiss them and take them into soft, pillowy beds to sleep tight in their arms. . . . But how could it be a merry Christmas for her, Florabelle thought. She had been looking forward to it so much, and now she was only a leftover, an extra. . . . Her glass eyes stared at the fire sadly and the clock on the mantel hurried along—*tick-tock, ticktock, ticktock—*

2

The Girl Who Could Talk to Dolls

"What are they doing?" asked the doll with her face to the wall. "I can't see a thing."

"They are wrapping the dolls," Florabelle said. Her voice trembled with sadness.

"How I wish I could see. You can't imagine how much I miss with my head on wrong," the little doll said. "My name is Lily—what's yours?"

"Florabelle."

"That's very nice," said Lily.

For a while the two sat in silence. Florabelle watched Miss Lavender and Miss Plum finish wrapping the dolls. Then the dolls were put back into the brown cardboard box and Miss Lavender and Miss Plum pushed it across the floor and hid it in the closet. On Christmas Eve, when all the little girls were sleeping, Miss Lavender and Miss Plum would take out the dolls and put them under the Christmas tree.

"There, that's done," Miss Plum said with satisfaction. She took a list out of her pocket and checked off *"Wrap dolls"* with a sharp black pencil.

"Yes, indeed," Miss Lavender agreed. "Won't the girls be happy when they see all these lovely dolls."

Then Miss Plum went off to see about some of the other "things-to-do" that she had written down on her list, and Miss Lavender sat down at the table again and began to sew angel wings on one of the costumes she picked up from the sofa. The room was very still.

"Now what are they doing?" Lily asked.

"They've finished wrapping the dolls and have put them away in the closet," Florabelle said.

"Aren't they going to wrap us?" Lily asked. Her voice was full of longing to be wrapped in Christmas paper and given to some little girl on Christmas morning. "Aren't they going to fix me and wrap me up, too?"

"I guess not right now, anyway," Florabelle answered. "We're extra."

"Well, this is just awful," Lily muttered to herself, staring grimly at the yellow flowers twining in the green wallpaper above the bookcase. "This is just awful! What's that? Now what's happening?"

"Some little girls are coming in," Florabelle said.

There had been a polite knock on the parlor door, and Miss Lavender had called "Come in" as well as she could with a row of pins lined up in her mouth. She looked up over her glasses as the door opened.

Five little girls wearing dark blue dresses with white collars, long black stockings, and black shoes with buckles at the sides—all exactly alike—came into the room.

Miss Lavender stood up, gathering the pins from her mouth and putting them back into her sewing basket.

"I've been expecting you," she said to the girls; and taking them one by one by the shoulder she lined them up in a row in front of the fireplace. "Now, who's missing?" she asked, and counted them off carefully:

"The Angel of Light. The Angel of Love. The

Angel of Hope. The Angel of Joy. The Angel of Peace on Earth—ah, now where is the Angel of Glory?"

As Miss Lavender had called off the names of the angels, each little girl had nodded her head, and it was only too plain to see that one was missing.

"It's Tatty," Miss Lavender said, looking closely at the five little girls. "Well, she'll probably be along—" And just as she spoke, a sixth little girl did appear in the parlor doorway. Her blue dress and white collar were just like the other little girls', and her black stockings and black shoes with buckles at the sides were just the same, but she did not, somehow, look quite as neat. Her long stockings had begun to collect down around her ankles and needed a good pull up, and her long straight brown hair fell forward into her eyes.

"Well, Tatty—come along, dear," Miss Lavender said. She began to hand out angel costumes to the little girls. "Here you are, Mary, and here you are, Emmy—and Cissie—and here's your costume, Elizabeth—and this one is Little Ann's—"

One by one the Angels of Light, Love, Hope, Joy, and Peace on Earth took the white flimsy floaty angel dresses and pairs of stiff white net wings. Then Miss Lavender said, "Now take these to the playroom—that will be our dressing room on the night of the program."

"Yes, Miss Lavender." "Yes, ma'am." And the five girls scampered off. Little Ann, the last one, the Angel of Peace on Earth, could not keep her costume from dragging along the floor, and she just missed catching it and tearing it on the woodbox by the fireplace. The stiff white angel wings stood up in front of her face, so she could hardly see where she was going, and she barely missed bumping into the doorway.

Only Tatty remained. Miss Lavender pulled up Tatty's stockings with a good tight yank at both knees, and smoothed the hair back from Tatty's forehead. Florabelle, the rag doll, watching from the top of the bookcase, was interested to see two large brown eyes appear from under the hair—and more surprised to see that the eyes were staring straight at her.

"Ohhh, Miss Lavender, look at the dolls," Tatty said.

Miss Lavender looked flustered. She and Miss Plum had not meant to leave even these two extra dolls where the girls might see them. It was so hard to remember to hide things away at Christmastime. Miss Lavender pretended to be very busy with the wings on Tatty's costume. "These wings are not even, I'm afraid—" she mumbled to herself.

"Are they your dolls?" Tatty asked.

"Dolls?—dolls?—I don't see any dolls," Miss Lavender muttered. She turned Tatty around and held the costume up to her back to see if the wings were even.

When she let go, Tatty turned around again.

"The dolls on the bookcase," Tatty said. She ran across the room and stretched up as far as she could reach. The bookcase was almost too high, but she did get hold of one of Florabelle's shoeless feet, and pulled her down by one leg.

"Woops!" Florabelle said.

"Woops!" Tatty echoed.

"Um—now—now—" Miss Lavender came over

to the bookcase. "These are just some old dolls that need some mending and fixing up—they aren't ready to play with yet. See, this one needs some shoes. And that other one needs some hair."

"And her head's on backward," Tatty said.

"Yes, her head's on backward," Miss Lavender said. She tried to distract Tatty's attention by holding up the angel costume again.

"When they're fixed up, whose dolls will they be?" Tatty wanted to know.

"Well, I—I don't know—" Miss Lavender fumbled for words.

"Oh, Miss Lavender—could they be mine?" Tatty begged. Her hair had begun to fall back across her forehead, and from under the fringe of straggling ends she stared up at Miss Lavender with such a beseeching expression that Miss Lavender could not think what to say.

"Well—ahem—" Miss Lavender cleared her throat to give herself time to think. She wished Miss Plum would come in; Miss Plum would know just the right thing to say.

"I don't have any dolls," Tatty said. "Oh,

couldn't I please have these? I like them so much."

"Oh, now, now." Miss Lavender laughed a little. "Why, how do you know what you'll find on Christmas morning—why, maybe on Christmas morning you will have a doll . . ." Miss Lavender's voice drifted off. Already she had said too much. But Tatty did not seem to understand.

"Oh, please, Miss Lavender," she begged again.

"Besides," Miss Lavender said, "this one's only a rag doll."

"But I like her," Tatty said. She held Florabelle very tightly and rocked her in her arms. "I like rag dolls *best*. They're so soft to hold."

"I like you, too," Florabelle said. She wished she could stay with Tatty forever. What a happy Christmas that would be!

"What's your name?" asked Tatty.

"Florabelle," the rag doll answered, although she did not expect much from this. Whenever people asked dolls what their names were, it was only to be polite, for they could never hear what the dolls answered.

But Tatty said, "Florabelle? That's pretty."

"My name is Lily," called the other doll from the top of the bookcase.

"Hello, Lily," Tatty said, looking up through her tangled hair at the back of the bald head of the doll above her.

Miss Lavender could not hear anything except what Tatty said. "Now, Tatty," she said, "stop playing; we must get this costume fixed."

Miss Lavender took Florabelle and put her back on the bookcase beside Lily. "Come over here by the sofa now, Tatty, and let me see if we can get the wings on your costume right."

Tatty allowed herself to be brought back to the sofa and the fireplace, but while Miss Lavender held the costume and pinned the wings here and there, Tatty kept looking over at Florabelle and Lily. When the wings were straight, Miss Lavender sewed them onto the costume with strong white thread. Tatty kept looking at Florabelle and Lily— and, at last, when Miss Lavender said the wings were finished and Tatty could go, Florabelle cried, "Oh, don't go—don't go—" Tatty lingered in the doorway, holding her costume under her arm, and then she said, "I'll come back and see you again soon."

Then she was gone, and the parlor door closed behind her.

"What's happening now?" Lily cried. "Has she gone?"

"Yes," Florabelle said wistfully, "she's gone."

"Do you think she *will* come back to see us?"

"Oh, I hope so," Florabelle said.

The door opened again, but it was only Miss Plum. Behind her came two girls about eleven or twelve years old, carrying a box of Christmas tree lights. Florabelle watched as they began to put lights and ornaments on the tree. The girls wore dark blue dresses and white collars and black shoes and stockings like the little girls who had carried off the angel costumes; but these girls were older and taller, tall enough to reach even the top branches of the Christmas tree. They did not have to get a chair to stand on, until it was time to put the silver star at the very top point of the tree.

While the girls were working, Miss Lavender drew Miss Plum aside.

"Tatty wanted those dolls over there. We forgot to put them out of sight. I almost told her she would have her own doll if she could be patient enough to wait until Christmas."

"But what will we do with these two?" Miss Plum murmured to herself. Miss Lavender shook her head to show that she did not know at all what they should do with Florabelle and Lily.

Then through the window Miss Plum saw a car stopping in front of The Good Day. She folded her hands tightly in front of her stomach. "We'll have to think about the dolls later. Mr. Not So Much is here."

And with that, Miss Lavender clasped *her* hands together, too, and looked very unhappy and flustered, and scurried after Miss Plum out of the parlor and down the hall to the front door, where a loud knocking could already be heard.

3

Mr. Not So Much

Florabelle and Lily could hear the sound of the front door opening and voices in the hall and then footsteps coming back along the hall toward the parlor.

"What's happening? What's happening?" Lily asked.

Miss Lavender and Miss Plum reappeared in the parlor, followed by a very tall thin man with a long thin face and a long thin nose. He had a watch in his pocket and a long gold chain, and he carried his hat in his hand.

"A gentleman has come to visit, I guess," Flora-belle said to Lilly.

"What does he look like?" Lily wanted to know.

The man had taken off his coat, and Miss Lavender was fluttering around brushing snowflakes off the coat collar and looking for a good spot to put the coat. Miss Plum seated herself on the sofa by the fire and the man sat down in a chair opposite the sofa, stiffly, as though he thought his legs would break if he bent his knees too deeply. He looked with disapproval at the girls who were hanging strands of silver icicles on the tree. "Not so much," he said, "not so much." Then he said to Miss Plum, "I hope you save the icicles from year to year. Every penny counts, you know. Can't run things on wasteful ways."

"How true," said Miss Plum. Miss Lavender looked over at the girls and smiled feebly. The girls began to roll their eyes and make faces when the grown-ups were not looking. One of the girls put a shiny icicle on her nose and blew it away.

"What does he look like?" Lily asked again, impatiently.

"He looks very stern," Florabelle said. "He's very thin and very stern looking, and he is dressed all in black."

"Oh," said Lily suddenly. "I think I'm afraid of him."

"How can you possibly be afraid of him when you haven't seen him?" Florabelle wanted to know.

"His voice sounds so cross and mean," Lily said. She lowered her own voice to a whisper, though of course there was no need, since none of the people in the room could hear dolls talk.

"A penny saved, ladies, is a penny earned," the visitor went on solemnly. He looked very grave. Then he said, "Too much wood on that fire, ladies. You must understand that we cannot have these spendthrift ways. Not so much wood, not so much wood."

Miss Lavender and Miss Plum looked guiltily toward their little fire—which Miss Lavender had only now been thinking really needed another good log. Mr. Not So Much was on the Board of Directors of The Good Day and he came once a month to check on things for the other directors. If Miss Lavender and Miss Plum had remembered this was his day, they would not have lit the fire at all.

Before Mr. Not So Much could find anything else to complain about, the door opened and one of the girls who was helping in the kitchen that afternoon came in with a tray of tea-things which Cook had just prepared.

"These are muffins the girls themselves made only this morning," Miss Lavender told Mr. Not So Much proudly. She poured a cup of tea for him, and waited to hear what he thought of the muffins.

"Too many raisins," he said. "Can't have that, you know." The girl who had brought in the tea tray turned pale as Mr. Not So Much fixed his burning black eyes upon her and repeated, "Can't have that, you know. Can't have these wasteful ways. Something will have to be done." Then to Miss Lavender and Miss Plum he said, "A penny saved, ladies, is a penny earned."

"Yes—yes—" Miss Plum motioned to the girl to go away *please,* and the girl hurried out of the parlor as fast as she could go. At the doorway she nearly bumped into Tatty and Little Ann, who had put on their angel costumes and come to show Miss Lavender and Miss Plum how nice they looked. They came running in, holding up the fronts of their angel skirts so they would not trip; beneath the gauzy white skirts their black stockings and sturdy black shoes stuck out.

"What is this?" Mr. Not So Much almost rose from his chair in his agitation to see the strange sight before him.

"What is it, what is it?" Lily asked Florabelle.

But Florabelle did not have to answer, for Lily could hear what Miss Plum was saying.

"Why, this is Little Ann," Miss Plum said, as calmly as she could, "and this is Tatty— Run along now, children." She was wishing Tatty and Little Ann would run along before Mr. Not So Much noticed their costumes—but, of course, he had noticed those the first thing. The costumes were the first thing anyone would notice, for they covered Tatty and Little Ann from head to foot, and behind each girl flapped two large net wings.

"But what *is* this?" Mr. Not So Much repeated,

setting down his cup of tea and the muffin with too many raisins. The girls trimming the Christmas tree began to giggle behind their hands.

"Why—these are costumes for our Christmas Eve program," Miss Plum explained. She tried to sound very unconcerned.

"All the girls in the program have one," Tatty said timidly. Miss Lavender and Miss Plum closed their eyes. There was no use worrying now; the worst was out.

"So all the girls in the program have a costume, do they?" Mr. Not So Much said. He stood up, pulled down his vest grimly, clasped his hands behind his back, and began to pace the floor like a long thin old bird.

"Oh, I *am* afraid of him, I *am*," Lily whispered to Florabelle—and this time Florabelle was not so sure she wasn't afraid, too.

"It obviously does no good to talk to you of saving and economizing, ladies." (Miss Lavender and Miss Plum shrank together on the sofa and looked up over their teacups helplessly.) "Each time I come," said Mr. Not So Much, "I find fresh evidence of squandering and spending of which I cannot dream. Fires burning—lamps lighted in every room—enough ornaments to trim a dozen trees—muffins so full of raisins there's hardly any muffin. Now each girl has a costume, a *cos*—tume." He drew the word out until even the doll Lily, who could not see him, shuddered just to hear. Tatty and Little Ann stared up at Mr. Not So Much, wide-eyed with fright.

"And I suppose," continued the director—and thinking wildly for some last fantastic fact to prove his case, he swung around and pulled open the closet door—"and I suppose the closet is full to the ceiling with Christmas toys!"

Little Ann and Tatty in their angel costumes and the girls trimming the tree craned their necks to look into the closet, but there was nothing to see there but some umbrellas and Miss Lavender's violin case and a big brown cardboard box.

"Well—anyway—" Mr. Not So Much closed the closet door crossly "—you know what I mean." The children looked very disappointed that he had not been right.

Miss Lavender and Miss Plum stole sly sideways glances of relief that the director had not thought to ask what was in the cardboard box while the girls were there. That would have spoiled the nice surprise.

At last Miss Plum said, as politely as she could, "Sir, there are many ways that we do economize. All the girls clean their own rooms; think of the savings there. And some of the girls help with the washing and ironing, and the younger ones help set the table and wipe the dishes."

Mr. Not So Much was making gestures to show that he didn't think these things counted for much at all.

"There must be some changes, must be some changes," he declared darkly, and peered around to see what he might find then and there to change.

Miss Plum went on, however. "And Cook is very careful when she does the marketing. Every penny spent on food is repaid by full value, I assure you. And I myself am teaching the girls how to play the piano. Think of the savings there."

"Having a piano at all is pure extravagance,"

Mr. Not So Much said, rapping the instrument sharply with his bony old knuckles, which set the metronome off—*click click click click click*—

"Stop that thing!" Mr. Not So Much exclaimed, and Miss Lavender bustled over, skirts flouncing out around her plump short legs, white curls bouncing. She clapped her hand over the ticking metronome. Tatty drew back fearfully, and Little Ann hid behind Tatty.

"And we are very sparing with our wood," Miss Plum went on, though she had paled considerably when Mr. Not So Much hit the piano. The piano was her pride and joy. How could they have music for all their nice programs if she could not play the piano while Miss Lavender played the violin? Miss Plum wanted to get the director's mind off the piano as quickly as possible, and the fire was the first thing she thought of.

"We have a fire this afternoon because it is so close to Christmas," she said. "It just seemed the right thing to do."

"Ah—I suppose you will be running off to the shops one of these days to buy yourself a diamond ring—and one for every girl"—he swept out his arm grandly—"because it seems the right thing to do."

At last Miss Plum could think of nothing more to say, and Miss Lavender stood rooted by the piano, her hand holding the metronome, her eyes, as round as saucers, fixed upon Mr. Not So Much.

"Ah!" He flung his hands out to show that he gave up. "It is of no use, ladies." Florabelle thought he was going to say a penny saved was a penny earned, but he said, "Waste not, want not!" Then he put on his hat, seized his coat, and went out into the hall again. Miss Plum rose and followed after, and Miss Lavender, securing the hand of the metronome, followed after Miss Plum. Trailing them all went Tatty and Little Ann, the Angel of Glory and the Angel of Peace on Earth.

By and by Florabelle could see Mr. Not So Much pass the parlor window on his way back to his car. The snow was coming down harder now, and he had his head lowered against it, his hand holding on to his hat. The wind whipped his coat out behind him like a great black cape.

"I hope we never meet him again!" said Lily.

4

A Terrible Thing!

"Well, that's over for another month," Miss Plum said, coming back into the parlor. Miss Lavender came nervously behind her, not yet fully recovered from the visit.

"Do you think he will make some changes?" Miss Lavender asked. She half expected the fireplace or the Christmas tree or the piano to suddenly disappear in a puff of smoke.

36

"He has been saying that for twenty years," Miss Plum reminded Miss Lavender.

"Yes, I know," Miss Lavender said. She felt somewhat reassured to recall that Mr. Not So Much had indeed been saying the same thing for twenty years, and nothing too bad had ever happened because of it.

"Let's not worry about him anymore today," Miss Plum said. "Let us just sit down and finish our tea and eat some muffins. We deserve them after all we've done today."

"Yes, you're right," Miss Lavender agreed. "I am simply worn out with wrapping Christmas dolls and sewing angel costumes, and everything." She sank into the sofa pillows, and they made a soft, squishy sound as she settled back.

There were four muffins left on the tray. Miss Plum put two on her own plate and two on Miss Lavender's plate, and they ate them up, raisins and all.

"Very good muffins," said Miss Plum.

"Oh, excellent," said Miss Lavender.

"Let's have another log on the fire," Miss Plum

suggested, and Miss Lavender hurried over and put a good extra-big log into the fireplace.

The afternoon had grown quite dark, and flakes of snow flung themselves upon the windowpanes. In the street beyond, cars sped past the black iron gate of Number 18 Butterfield Square. From somewhere in the rooms above, Florabelle and Lily could hear little girls singing ". . . *Jingle bells, jingle bells, jingle all the way . . . Oh, what fun it is to ride . . . in a one horse open . . . sleigh-eigh . . .*"

"I can smell gingerbread baking," Lily said. "At the house where I used to live, the children's mother made gingerbread every Saturday. It smelled so good. She put white icing on, and the children took turns licking the icing bowl, one each Saturday. My, I wish I were there now."

Lily's voice faded off sadly, and Florabelle said, "Don't feel bad, Lily. This seems like a nice place. By and by they will fix your head and get you some hair, and everything will be all right."

"I hope so," the little bald-headed doll answered with a sigh. "I just can't help feeling homesick sometimes." Then after a moment she asked, "What was your home like, Florabelle? Before you came here, I mean."

"I never had a home," Florabelle said. "I always lived in a toy shop."

"You never had a home?" Lily asked. She was quite surprised.

"No," said Florabelle. "I've always wanted to belong to a little girl, but no one ever bought me. Then one day the toy-shop owner took me off the shelf and put me in a drawer behind the counter. He said he didn't think anyone was ever going to buy me, and his wife said I didn't look very fresh anymore."

"That wasn't a very nice thing to say," Lily interrupted.

"I suppose it was true," Florabelle admitted. "I'd been sitting on that toy-shop shelf so long, I just didn't look new and fresh anymore. I was dusty, and see how my dress is faded."

"I can't see anything but this wallpaper," Lily reminded her. "There are six flowers in each circle, and five leaves on each stem, and eight petals on each flower." Florabelle could see Lily had been memorizing the wallpaper pattern.

"How did you get to the clock factory?" Lily asked next.

"The toy-shop owner donated me, with a big box of other toys, just like those other dolls were donated by children who had new dolls to play with or had grown up and gotten tired of playing with toys."

"That's what happened to me," Lily said. "One day the children's mother said, 'Now let's get together some toys you don't play with much anymore and Daddy will take them to the factory tomorrow.' The children's daddy worked at the clock factory, you see."

"What happened to your hair and your head?" Florabelle asked.

"Well," said Lily, "my hair had been missing for a long time. No one seemed to know where it had gone. You see, it came unglued—wigs sometimes do, you know—and before the children's mother could get around to gluing it back on, it got lost somewhere. Then one day my head began to get loose, and one of the children turned it around backward for fun, and it wouldn't turn back. It's been quite a nuisance—and I don't suppose I look very pretty either, without my hair. It was lovely brown hair, with curls and ribbons."

"It sounds lovely," Florabelle said softly. "My hair is only yarn."

"Is it?" Lily said. "Well, don't complain. Yarn hair is better than none, I can tell you that. And anything's better than having your head on wrong."

While the dolls were talking, Miss Lavender and Miss Plum had finished their tea. Miss Lavender carried away the tray, while Miss Plum tidied up the table where they had been wrapping the Christmas dolls and working on the angel costumes. The fire had died out. The clock on the mantel chimed six o'clock, and Lily said, "Must be suppertime."

"I guess so," Florabelle said. "I can smell something awfully good cooking somewhere."

Miss Plum gave a last look around the room, and caught sight of the two dolls on the top of the bookcase. She came over and picked up Lily and began to examine her head to see if she could twist it around frontward again. As she turned the little doll, a trickle of sawdust fell down to the floor. Miss Plum examined Lily more closely and found a place that was coming apart where Lily's smooth pink arm joined her cloth body.

"Hmmm," said Miss Plum, "I hardly think this doll's worth fixing." And to the horror of the dolls, Miss Plum dropped Lily into the wastepaper basket by the table. In she sank among the scraps of Christmas paper and pieces of thread from the sewing basket.

"*Oh—no—wait—wait—*" Lily cried as loudly as she could.

Florabelle cried, "*Oh—oh—don't do that!*"

But of course Miss Plum did not hear Lily or Florabelle. Miss Plum looked at the things on the table again and then threw a piece of letter paper into the wastebasket. It landed on Lily and covered her like a sleek white blanket.

Lily had fallen on her stomach, so her face was upward, and as she stared from the dark steep sides of the wastepaper basket to the ceiling above, she saw Miss Plum's hand appear again—and this time Miss Plum threw in a crumpled-up ball of tissue paper scraps. This landed right on Lily's face, so she could see no more. But she knew that Miss Plum had turned out the lights and gone away, for everything got dark and she heard a door closing and footsteps fading away along the hall.

5

Out Into the Night

The next morning Florabelle, the rag doll, could see only a beautiful white world through the parlor window. Even the cars creeping slowly along in the street were covered with snow, like frosted buns, and each branch of each tree was white with snow. It was like fairyland, Florabelle thought—and now the very next day was Christmas. Although she feared she might not get to be some little girl's Christmas present, Florabelle felt even sorrier for Lily, lying alone in the wastepaper basket.

It was too far from the top of the bookcase across the room to the bottom of the wastepaper basket for the dolls to talk much, but every once in a while Florabelle would shout down, "I'm still here, Lily. Don't worry, everything will be all right."

"No—this is the end of me for sure," Lily would call back. Her voice was muffled by the ball of paper lying on her face.

Miss Lavender and Miss Plum came into the parlor about the middle of the morning, and brought the two girls who had been trimming the tree. Together they all cleaned up the parlor and set out some folding chairs at one side. They moved all the chairs and lamps and the big table away from the windows, so there was a large empty space which would be the stage. When the parlor was all ready for the Christmas Eve program, everyone went away again. Miss Plum was the last to go. She took out her key, and when she went she locked the door behind her so that none of the children could get into the parlor and disturb anything while it was all fixed up for the program.

Slowly the day passed. Steadily the clock on the mantel ticked, steadily it chimed the passing hours. Sorrowfully Florabelle watched the cars and the people going by outside. The people carried Christmas packages and hurried along, smiling and happy; it was the day before Christmas—a wonderful, wonderful day.

Except for Florabelle, and poor Lily in the wastepaper basket.

The afternoon was drawing to a close, when Miss Plum reappeared. Florabelle heard her key at the lock of the parlor door, and she came in carrying another brown cardboard carton which had just come by parcel post for the little girls. The box was full of smaller boxes, each one stuffed with candy and nuts, and Miss Plum hid this all away in the closet with the big box of Christmas dolls. Then she sat down at the table and took her list out of her pocket and began to check over the things she had done and the things she had yet to do.

The top of the paper said *"Trim tree,"* and that was checked off. The next thing was *"Wrap dolls,"* and that was checked off. Farther down the list were items like *"Oranges and apples for stockings,"* and *"Turkey,"* *"Stuffing,"* and *"Plum pudding."*

It was a long list, and before Miss Plum got to the end, checking and thinking and making notes to herself in the margin, her head began to nod, and at last she leaned back in the chair. Her eyes closed. Her head tipped sideways. The pencil slipped from her fingers, rolled along the floor, and came to a stop beside a sofa leg.

By and by there was a soft rapping on the parlor door, which stood ajar. When Miss Plum, soundly asleep now, did not answer, a face came round the door—a tiny face with large dark eyes almost hidden by straggling hair. It was Tatty, come to see the dolls. Because she could see Miss Plum was sleeping, she did not disturb her, but tiptoed to the bookcase and reached up for Florabelle.

"I told you I would come back to see you," she said. "Why—where is Lily?"

"Oh, I am so glad you've come," Florabelle

cried. Her voice quavered with sadness and happiness together. "Lily is in the wastepaper basket. She's been thrown away."

"Thrown away?" Tatty said. She held Florabelle closer and tighter, as if she might lose her, too, somehow.

"Miss Plum said she was not worth fixing. Besides her head on backward and her hair gone, she's got a leak in her sawdust somewhere."

Tatty tiptoed past the table. Miss Plum stirred a little, but went on nodding and dozing. Tatty looked into the wastebasket and saw only paper at first. She took the rim of the basket in one hand and jiggled the basket carefully. The ball of tissue paper rolled away from Lily's face—and she stared up at Tatty from the midst of the scraps. Tatty's eyes widened as she stared back down at the doll.

"Oh, dear," Tatty said to Florabelle, "you're right!"

"Can't you help us?" Florabelle pleaded.

Tatty reached into the wastepaper basket and lifted up Lily.

"Poor Lily," she said, hugging her close. Flora-

belle and Lily thought it was wonderful for Tatty to be hugging them so tight and loving them so much. They wished they could stay with her forever.

"I'll take you to a toy shop," Tatty said suddenly. Her face lighted up with this idea. "We'll get you all fixed up, Lily. Then no one will want to throw you away."

"What about me?" Florabelle begged. "Don't leave me here, please—they'll throw me away next; I know they will."

Tatty did not look quite sure what to do about Florabelle. In her desperation not to be left behind, Florabelle made things sound worse than they really were. "They don't like rag dolls," she said to Tatty, and when she saw that Tatty was somewhat moved by this, she quickly added, "When they first saw me they said 'Ugh, a horrid old rag doll!'"

"Shame on you, Florabelle," Lily whispered. "They didn't say it like that at all."

But Lily said this very softly, so that Tatty did not notice. Then Lily said more loudly to Tatty, "Please don't leave Florabelle. She's my friend."

"Well . . ." said Tatty slowly, looking back and forth from the dolls to Miss Plum, dozing in the chair by the table. "If they really don't like rag dolls, I guess they won't mind if I take you, will they?"

"They'll be very relieved not to have me sitting around," Florabelle urged. She was afraid Miss Plum would wake up at any second and stop Tatty from taking her away. She wanted to belong to Tatty more than anything else in the world.

"All right," said Tatty, "I'll take you with me, for right now, anyway." She began to tiptoe from the room. Miss Plum started in her sleep, but then sank back again and began to snore softly into her collar.

In the hall, Tatty got her coat and scarf and mittens from a long closet lined with little coats and scarves and mittens all exactly alike. Below each coat, on the closet floor, was a pair of boots. Tatty put on everything as quickly as she could, and Florabelle and Lily sat on the floor among the boots urging her to hurry. They were afraid Miss Plum would waken and find them gone—or Miss

Lavender might come along—or one of the big girls—or Cook—or—

And then somebody did come along—Little Ann, the Angel of Peace on Earth, and Mary, the Angel of Light.

"Tatty! What are you doing?" Mary exclaimed. It was time to wash up for supper, not time to be putting on coats and scarves and mittens and boots.

"I have to go out," Tatty said.

"Aren't you ever coming back?" asked Little Ann. She was the smallest of all the little girls. Someone had found a scrap of Christmas ribbon and tied it around her soft yellow hair, but the bow had slipped down over one ear.

"Of course I'm coming back," Tatty said. "I'm just going out for a minute. I'll be right back."

"Did Miss Plum say you could go?" Mary asked.

Of course Miss Plum had not said she could go. Miss Plum was sleeping. No one had said she could go. . . . "I'll be right back," Tatty said again.

"Will you be back in time for supper?" Mary asked. She had red hair and freckles and round red cheeks. She was eating a cookie and her mouth was covered with crumbs.

"I—I don't know—" Tatty hesitated. It was nearly suppertime now, and she was very hungry. Seeing Mary eating her cookie made Tatty feel even hungrier.

"Don't miss supper," said Little Ann. "We're having everything good, and cake for dessert."

"The cake has pink frosting—this thick," said Mary. She held up her thumb and first finger quite far apart. "We peeked."

"I'll try to be back in time for supper," Tatty said. She had put on all her wraps now, and she picked up the dolls.

"Where did you get the dolls?" Mary asked.

"That one has no hair," said Little Ann.

"I have to hurry," Tatty said. She started toward the big front door.

"Well, good-bye," said Little Ann.

Mary ate the last of her cookie and dusted the cookie crumbs from her mouth. "What about the program?" she asked. "You won't miss our Christmas Eve program, will you, Tatty?"

"No, of course not," said Tatty.

As she went to the door, Little Ann and Mary hovered behind her, and as she went out they called after her to hurry back in time for the program because she was the Angel of Glory.

When the door closed behind Tatty, the patch of light was gone, and everything looked very cold and dark. Dusk had fallen, and the streetlamps were going on around Butterfield Square. It had begun to snow again and the flakes drifted down against the dolls' faces. They waited silently for Tatty to decide which way to go. Tatty did not seem to be very sure. She was only seven years old, and she had never gone out to a shop alone before.

She went down the steps and out to the street. By the black iron gate she stopped and looked both ways along the street. People hurrying by paid no attention to her.

At last Florabelle said, "Do you know where a toy shop is, Tatty?"

"No—" Tatty admitted, "but we'll find one."

And she set off at last along the street, into the snow and the gathering darkness.

6

The Toyman

Tatty did not have to walk far before she came to a street lined with shops. Every window was ablaze with Christmas lights and sparkling with Christmas decorations. There was a shoe store and a stationery shop, a grocery store and a bakery, a record shop, a dress shop, a book shop, and a candy shop. The street was crowded with people hurrying to finish their errands and get home. It was Christmas Eve, and everyone wanted to be out of the cold and snow, cozy in their warm houses, enjoying their beautiful Christmas trees or wrapping their Christmas gifts.

"Oh, dear," Tatty said to Florabelle and Lily. "I don't seem to see any toy shops—do you?"

Florabelle and Lily looked out from under Tatty's arm. Snowflakes flew in their faces, and melted on Florabelle's green glass-button eyes. Everything looked wet to her after that, as if she were looking at the world under water. At the street corner a lady in a long cape stood ringing a brass bell, and in one store window there was a scene of Christmas carolers made of dolls in old-fashioned clothes. *"Deck the halls with boughs of holly, fa la la la la, la la la la. . . ."* The song came out through a loudspeaker to the people in front of the store window.

It was all very bright and lovely to see. Tatty went along looking at all the shopwindows and listening to the bells and the songs. She would have liked to have stopped at every shopwindow to look more closely at the pretty things, but she wanted to be back before Miss Plum woke up. She wanted to be back before anyone missed her. The dusk was deepening. Soon it would be really dark.

"We must hurry," someone said, jostling past

Tatty on the crowded street. "The stores will all be closing soon."

"Did you hear that?" Florabelle called to Tatty. "The stores will be closing soon!"

"I never thought of that," Tatty said. Her dark eyes clouded unhappily. "We must find a toy shop before it closes."

"There's one!" Lily cried suddenly. "There, straight ahead. See the dolls and toy soldiers in the window!"

And, at last, there before them was a toy shop. But as Tatty ran toward it a man appeared at the doorway and drew down a shade over the door. When it was down Tatty could read that it said CLOSED in very big letters. She knocked at the door as loudly as she could, and the shade came up a few inches and the man peeked out at her. Then he disappeared and Tatty and the dolls heard him clicking back the lock on the door. A moment later the door opened and the man stood looking down at them, a towering man with dark curly hair.

"Why, what's this?" he asked—for right away he noticed Lily's pink bald head and he knew that something was wrong. He held the door open, and Tatty stepped in. Oh, it was warm and bright in the toy shop.

"Is this your toy shop, Florabelle?" Lily asked.

"No," Florabelle replied. "But it's quite a bit like it. Toy shops seem to be rather the same, now that I see another one." She looked around at the shelves lined with toys, so much like the shelf she had sat upon, unbought, for so many months.

"Now, what can I do for you, young lady?" the shopkeeper asked, and Tatty told him, all in a burst, about poor Lily being thrown away because she had no hair and her head was on backward.

"And she has a leak in her sawdust," Florabelle added.

"Yes," Tatty told the man, "—a leak in her stuffing."

Poor Lily listened silently. She found that now she was rather embarrassed to have so many things wrong with her. And as though to make matters worse, the toyman himself said, "And she has no shoes, either."

"Can't we fix her up?" Tatty begged. "She is

such a pretty doll, and I know she will be sad to be thrown away. Her name is Lily."

"Lily, eh?" The toyman took Lily in his large hands, very gently and carefully. Then he lifted Tatty up and set her down on the counter right beside him so she could see what he was going to do. Florabelle snuggled in Tatty's lap, and Tatty wiped Florabelle's eyes dry, so she could see everything better again.

First the toyman gave a good yank and took Lily's head off completely. Then with a large needle and stiff thread he sewed her head on again, right side around.

"Oh, this is such a relief," were Lily's first words.

Then the toyman looked in a big drawer behind the counter and found a wig that was the right size for Lily. It was a wig of black curls, tied at each side with tiny blue-silk ribbons.

"It's even more beautiful than the wig I had before!" Lily exclaimed with delight when she saw it.

After the toyman glued the wig firmly in place,

he took his stiff thread again and sewed up the hole by Lily's arm where the sawdust was spilling out. He wore a heavy silver ring which flashed in the light as he pulled the needle and thread back and forth. When he smiled, they could see that his teeth were all white but one, and that was a beautiful shining gold.

"Now I'm as good as new," Lily said, when the sewing was finished. "Surely no one would dream of throwing me away again. See how beautiful I am!"

"Don't be so vain," Florabelle scolded. "Besides, you still don't have any shoes."

"That's right," said Tatty to the shopkeeper. She forgot that he could not hear Florabelle or Lily himself.

"What's right?" he asked.

"She still doesn't have any shoes."

"We can fix that," the man said. He went to one of the shelves and took down a box full of cellophane packages of doll shoes.

"Oh," said Tatty, when she saw this, "I'm afraid I don't have any money."

"I never take money on Christmas Eve," the toyman answered, with a wink of one great dark eye. He opened one of the packages and put a pair of tiny white shoes with white silk laces on Lily's feet.

"Ohhh—this is more than I expected," Lily exclaimed, and she felt that she was even more beautiful than ever now.

Florabelle was glad to see her friend Lily fixed up so nicely, but she did feel a little dingy herself, now that Lily was so elegant. Of all the Christmas dolls, she was the only doll left without shoes.

Almost as if the toyman read her thoughts, he lifted Florabelle from Tatty's lap and said, "My goodness, none of your dolls have shoes, do they?"

"They're not exactly *my* dolls," Tatty said timidly, but the man was shuffling through the box of doll shoes, and this time he took out a shiny black pair with tiny black bows on the front. He put these on Florabelle's feet, and she thought surely no rag doll in all the world had ever had such splendid shiny shoes.

"Now, how's that?" The toyman set the dolls

side by side in front of him to take a good look at them. They smiled back as hard as they could, and wished he could hear them tell him how much they thanked him.

"Tell him how happy we are," Lily said to Tatty; and Tatty said to the toy-shop owner, "They are very happy and they want to thank you for everything."

"Do they, now?" The man lifted Tatty from the counter and set her on the floor. She put on her mittens, and he handed Florabelle and Lily to her. She tucked a doll under each arm, and walked with the man to the toy-shop door.

"Better hurry along home now, little one," the shopkeeper said. He opened the door for Tatty. "It's Christmas Eve, and you want to get home before it gets any later."

"Yes, sir," said Tatty. She started out, and then she turned back and said, "I have to hurry to get back in time for the program. I am going to be the Angel of Glory."

"Indeed." The man smiled down at her kindly. "I am sure you will make a very good angel."

"I have a white dress to wear," Tatty said. "And white wings on my back."

"Good-bye, little one," the shopkeeper said. He stood in the doorway and watched as Tatty walked away. She turned back once to wave, and the toy-man waved, too. "Merry Christmas," he called.

"Merry Christmas," called back Tatty and Florabelle and Lily. They all felt very happy.

But after they had turned the corner and the toy shop was out of sight, they began to wonder which way to go. All the shops looked alike, and all the streets looked the same. Some of the shops were closed up now, and there were not so many people out.

It had grown very dark, and much colder, and Tatty began to shiver. She held the dolls very tightly and tried to think which way would be best to go. She had never been out alone at night before. All the streets looked so much alike, and nothing looked very familiar to her.

"Are we lost?" Florabelle asked—but Tatty did not answer.

7

Where Is Tatty?

Meanwhile, back at Number 18 Butterfield Square it had at last been discovered that Tatty was missing.

Her absence would have been noticed much more quickly, except that everything was in such a bustle and buzz of excitement and preparation. Cook was busiest of all, fixing Christmas Eve supper. But she didn't mind at all being busy. She thought Christmas was the most wonderful time of the year, and she had put a sprig of holly on her apron front and a comb of imitation diamonds in her hair. When she had time from cooking, she admired herself in a mirror over the kitchen stove.

Just before it was time to eat, Cook put a red and white striped candy cane in front of every plate at the table—Tatty's too.

In came the little girls with their blue dresses and white collars, black shoes and black stockings. They did not come in very quietly, because it was hard to be quiet when they were so excited about Christmas. They could smell such wonderful, wonderful smells coming from the kitchen; and Mary had told everybody about the cake with the thick icing.

Miss Plum was still attending to some last-minute details in the parlor, but in came Miss Lavender and took her place at the end of the table. Her pile of white curls was freshly combed, and she had even used a little rouge (which she saved for special occasions). Her cheeks were very pink and beautiful.

The girls sat down, poking each other and eyeing the candy canes in front of the plates. But one chair was empty; one place had no little girl happy to see a candy cane waiting for her.

And so it was discovered that Tatty was missing.

"Now, where's Tatty?" Miss Lavender said, a little annoyed that now, of all times, someone should be out of place.

All the little girls turned to look at the empty chair.

"She's gone out, Miss Lavender," Mary said. And everyone looked at Mary then. She sat up straight and tried to look wise.

"Long, long ago," said Little Ann helpfully.

"Oh, wouldn't you know," said a big girl named Elsie May, who was twelve and could hardly bear the silly things that the little girls did. She stroked the new ribbons on her braids and stuck her nose in the air.

Miss Lavender had begun to look somewhat distressed when Mary said that Tatty had gone out. When Little Ann said "long, long ago," Miss Lavender began to look even more distressed. She took off her spectacles and waved them in the air.

"Long, long ago? Where did she go?"

But Mary and Little Ann did not know this.

"Oh!" Poor Miss Lavender. She put on her spectacles and looked all around the table to be sure that she did not see Tatty somewhere safely there after all.

"She just went out by herself," Mary said, shrugging her shoulders and staring at Miss Lavender with her round blue eyes.

Miss Lavender gazed at Mary as though she really could not believe her ears to hear such a dreadful thing.

"She went out *alone?*" Miss Lavender asked. "She went out *alone*—in the *snow?* In this *dark?* Oh, dear—oh, dear—oh, dear."

And she hurried away to tell Miss Plum.

Miss Plum knew exactly what to do, and she went straight to the telephone that hung in the hall at the foot of the stairway. She asked to be connected with the police station. The policeman who answered listened to Miss Plum and then he said that he would send someone over at once to find out the details.

Miss Plum told Miss Lavender this, and Miss Lavender said, "Find out the details? What more details do they need? Our dear little Tatty is out alone on this cold, dark night—oh, our poor dear little Tatty—" And Miss Lavender took off her spectacles and dabbed at her eyes with her handkerchief. Her plump pink face was trembling with dismay.

"How could she have gone out without asking," Miss Plum said with a sigh. "Well, now, Miss Lavender, don't worry so. The policeman will be here soon. He will take care of everything. Maybe someone will be able to think of where she might have gone."

In the meantime, the little girls were told to finish up their nice supper and get ready for the program. It seemed best to try to keep everything as nearly normal as possible. Miss Lavender and Miss Plum tried to think of where Tatty could have gone, so as to be of some help to the officer when he came around from the station. But try as they might, they could not think where she might have gone.

In the parlor the Christmas tree lights were turned on, and a fire burned merrily on the hearth. Soon the audience began to assemble in the folding chairs.

There were all the girls who were not in the program.

There were the handyman and his wife.

And Cook, with her holly sprig and diamond comb, and her little granddaughter, who always came to see the Christmas Eve programs. Cook's granddaughter was nine years old this year, and she sat very straight and quiet with her hands folded just so in her lap because she had a new dress to wear and her mother had said several times, "When you go to the program, please sit still and do not fidget or wrinkle your new dress."

There was also a nice old couple who lived across the Square and often came to visit, bringing homemade jelly and cookies for the little girls.

The scenery was in place. Large silver cardboard stars hung upon the curtains at the sides of the windows, and there was a large cardboard box painted gray and black to look like a great rock. One of the girls was dressed like a shepherd boy, and she was going to sit on the rock. Two other girls were dressed like sheep. The story of the shepherds abiding in the fields was the first part of the program. Then came the angels; and the last part was the singing of Christmas carols. Miss Plum was going to play the piano, and Miss Lavender was going to play the violin.

Miss Lavender and Miss Plum stood in the parlor doorway. The sight of all the lovely things, the fire burning and the glittering Christmas tree, the silver stars hanging on the curtains, only made Miss Lavender feel worse to think of Tatty out in the cold snowy night. Beyond the parlor windows, flakes of snow whirled through the light of the streetlamps.

"It's snowing harder than ever," Miss Lavender whispered to Miss Plum. "Harder than ever . . . oh, our poor little Tatty. . . ."

8

Lost

Tatty had to admit that they were lost. She held Florabelle and Lily very tightly and tried not to cry. She wondered if Miss Plum and Miss Lavender had noticed yet that she was gone. She wished they would notice, and come and look for her. But how could they find her? She had wandered a long way from the shops, and no street seemed to be the one that led to Butterfield Square. Cars went by silently in the snowy streets, and in the windows of houses Tatty could see the bright lights of Christmas trees. A chime sounded off in the distance somewhere, its notes hanging upon the air and echoing in the stillness.

"It must be very late," Florabelle said. Snowflakes had melted on her green glass-button eyes again, and her dress and yarn hair were damp with snow.

Lily was smaller and better protected under Tatty's arm, but even so her new black wig was dotted with snowflakes. "Oh, Tatty," Lily said, "I wonder if you've missed your supper."

"I guess I have," Tatty answered. She was very tired and hungry, and she wished she was back where she belonged having a nice supper and getting ready to be the Angel of Glory. She remembered how good Mary's cookie had looked as she stood eating it while Tatty put on her coat and boots. Little Ann had said they were going to have "everything good, and cake for dessert." "With icing this thick," Mary had said. Tatty felt so hungry she thought she could hardly stand it. It seemed as if she had been walking forever.

At last Tatty and the dolls came to a low stone wall, and beyond they could see a church, its steeple outlined against the dark and snowy sky. There were lights lit in the church, and they shone out through the colored glass windows and made beautiful colored pictures on the snow-covered lawn. The chimes they had heard before were coming from this church, and Tatty stood for a moment staring across the snow at the tall spire reaching up into the night.

"I'll bet you've even missed the program by now," Lily said sadly.

"I suppose I have," Tatty answered. She was tired and cold and hungry, and she had wanted so much to be the Angel of Glory. It was Christmas Eve and she was lost—who knew how far away by now she was from Miss Lavender and Miss Plum and all her friends.

There were people coming along the street and going into the church for the service, and Flora-belle said, "Maybe we could ask someone the way to Butterfield Square."

But the people were hurrying by quickly, and

no one seemed to pay any attention to Tatty and Florabelle and Lily.

"Well, let's just stay here a few minutes anyway and listen to the chimes," Florabelle said. She thought Tatty must be tired from walking so long, and it seemed she had tried as hard as she could to find the way. It was very beautiful near the church, and it did not seem so lonely there. The snow fell less and less rapidly, and finally stopped.

So they remained staring up at the church and the steeple rising against the dark Christmas sky above, listening to the chimes ring out into the night. And as they stood there, a man came walking along and stopped beside them. He, too, was looking at the church, though he was not on his way to the service and he only paused a moment. He did not even notice Tatty and the dolls.

"Look, Tatty," Florabelle cried. "It's Mr. Not So Much!"

Tatty looked up at the tall thin black figure beside her, and shrank away fearfully when she saw that it was, indeed, Mr. Not So Much.

"Is that really him?" whispered Lily. She had

had her face to the wallpaper when Mr. Not So Much had come into the parlor. Now that she saw what he looked like, she was more afraid of him than before. She thought he looked as cross and mean as he had sounded. "Maybe be won't see us," she added frantically. "Can't you find somewhere to hide, Tatty?"

But it seemed to Florabelle that Mr. Not So Much was better than nothing, and she said, "Couldn't we just ask him the way back? Surely he will know."

Tatty looked up at the forbidding figure beside her doubtfully, but before she could gather her courage to speak, he turned and strode away.

"Follow him," Florabelle urged.

"Oh, no," begged Lily. "Let's hide, let's hide!"

"Go on, Tatty," Florabelle urged again, "follow him—hurry—or we'll lose him."

Already Mr. Not So Much was disappearing from sight into the darkness.

9

"Please, Sir!"

Tatty started after the tall thin man, but his legs were so much longer than hers and he was stalking away so rapidly that she could not catch up with him. She ran as fast as she could, stumbling through the snow and bumping into people coming along the street to church.

At last she came up behind him. He had stopped at a street corner to wait for the traffic light to change, and a newsboy sprang from the shelter of a newsstand and waved a paper at Mr. Not So Much.

"Paper, sir? Late evening paper here."

"Go on with you," Mr. Not So Much snapped, with an impatient wave of his hand.

"Please, sir," began Tatty in a very tiny, timid voice.

"Go on with you." Mr. Not So Much did not even look at her, but waved her off with his hand and sped on across the street. Tatty trailed behind him, splashing in the slushy snow. When they were across to the other side she tried again, calling as loudly as she could:

"Please, sir!"

He turned and stared down at her crossly. "Well, what is it, what is it?"

"Please, sir," Tatty began again, "I'm from The Good Day, sir."

Mr. Not So Much bent down to examine her more closely.

"The Good Day?" he asked suspiciously. He could see that she was a little girl like the ones at

The Good Day, but of course he had never taken the time to notice what their faces were like.

"Yes, sir," Tatty replied. Her nose was beginning to run, and she sniffed and shivered with cold.

Mr. Not So Much was clearly exasperated.

"In that case, what are you doing *here?*" he demanded fiercely.

"I've been out—and now I'm lost," Tatty stammered.

Mr. Not So Much continued to stare at her crossly and suspiciously. Whatever she was out for, he seemed to be thinking, it could certainly be to no good.

"Did the ladies let you go out alone?" he asked next.

"Not exactly," Tatty said. "I had something to do, sort of like a surprise—" her voice trembled off, and her last words were drowned anyway by the loud tooting of a bus crossing the intersection.

A car honked back at the bus, and Mr. Not So Much said, "Bah! We can't talk here in the middle of all this confusion. Come, follow me, I will show you the way."

And he strode off again, muttering to himself about this inconvenient turn of events.

Tatty staggered along behind as well as she could, slipping on the snowy sidewalk, trying to keep up.

"Keep on, Tatty," Florabelle said. "Everything's going to be all right now." Tatty did not have the breath to answer. She was gasping and stumbling, sure that she had lost Mr. Not So Much among the people, when she saw him in front of her again, and hurrying to catch up once more she saw that he had stopped and was looking back at her. He was waiting for her, and then when she came up to him he reached out and took Tatty's hand. She held both dolls in the other arm, and it was much easier now to keep up, with Mr. Not So Much holding her securely by the hand. But she still had to run along.

Mr. Not So Much looked down every so often, and Tatty looked up at him and tried not to be so frightened of him.

And then Mr. Not So Much did another unexpected thing. He stopped again, and this time he lifted Tatty up into his arms, dolls and all, and walked along carrying her.

"Oh, oh, oh, oh," gasped Lily, who found her face pressed tight against Mr. Not So Much's shoulder. She thought she would probably never be the same again after such an experience!

10

Whom Do We Belong To Now?

Tatty and Mr. Not So Much, Florabelle and Lily, arrived at the door of The Good Day while Miss Plum was explaining the "details" of Tatty's disappearance to the policeman who had come around from the police station.

"She is seven years old," Miss Plum was saying, "and she is wearing a blue dress and a dark blue coat."

Miss Lavender had stayed in the parlor with the children, but she came to the parlor doorway and listened anxiously while Miss Plum spoke to the policeman. The children gave up waiting for the program to start. They clustered around the piano and Elsie May picked out "Jingle Bells" with one finger to show the other girls how clever she was.

When Mr. Not So Much knocked at the door, Miss Plum excused herself to the policeman and stepped over to open the door. When she saw that it was Tatty home safe and sound, she took her into her arms at once and called, "Miss Lavender! Miss Lavender! Tatty's here!"

Miss Lavender came flying out of the parlor, for she could already see for herself that Tatty was back. All the girls came clattering along behind Miss Lavender, except one small girl who had been watching her chance to have a turn at the piano; and she stayed behind to see if she could play "Jingle Bells."

After a great many exclamations and explanations, and then more explanations and exclamations, Miss Plum remembered the policeman. He had stepped aside politely to get out of the way of all the commotion, and was holding his hat in his hand.

"Gracious," Miss Plum said, when she remembered the policeman. "We won't be needing you after all!"

As much as Miss Plum and Miss Lavender tried to thank Mr. Not So Much, he only brushed them aside and said, "Not so much chatter. Not so much foolishness." And then when he went into the parlor and found the little girl who had stayed behind to play "Jingle Bells," he frowned at her from his great height and said, "Not so much noise, please."

At last everyone went back to getting ready for the program. Tatty was rushed into the kitchen to have a very fast supper and then rushed into the dressing room to put on her angel costume.

Miss Lavender put Florabelle and Lily on top of the piano, and there the dolls had a good view of the program and very much enjoyed the sound of the plinking piano keys just below them. They thought they had never had such an exciting time

in all their lives, and they took turns admiring each other's new shoes and remarking how things had worked out so nicely.

"I was never really worried a bit," Florabelle said airily. "I knew everything would be all right."

"I was never worried either," Lily said, just as airily. But then she added a little doubtfully, "Except, whom do we belong to now?"

Before Florabelle could think of an answer to that, Miss Plum clapped her hands together for attention. It was time for the program to begin.

When it was their turn, the six little girls who were angels came in from the hall where they had been waiting and peeking through the parlor door. They took their places by the curtains decorated with silver cardboard stars. Tatty was at the very end of the line. How happy she looked now; no tears or sniffly nose or pinched cold fingers and frozen cheeks . . . even her hair was nicely combed and held back neatly by a white ribbon. Her long angel dress covered everything but the very tips of her small black shoes. She looked like the most beautiful little girl in the world to Florabelle and Lily.

Miss Plum began to play "Silent Night" very softly on the piano.

"I am the Angel of Light," Mary said. "Heaven and earth are full of my radiance."

One by one the little girls said their lines:

"I am the Angel of Love, bringing to everyone my gifts of Hope, Joy, and Peace on Earth."

"I am the Angel of Hope. You may find me wherever you hear voices singing the carols of Christmas."

"I am the Angel of Joy. You may see me upon each face touched with the wonder of Christmas."

"I am the Angel of Peace on Earth," said Little Ann. "I live in the hearts of men, and wherever a heart receives me, there is Christmas."

Then it was Tatty's turn.

"I am the Angel of Glory," said Tatty, "filling all the earth with singing and rejoicing and praise to God, Christmas and forever."

Miss Lavender found it necessary to get out her handkerchief again and dab at her eyes, and Miss Plum sat up a little straighter at the piano and blinked a tear back from her own eyes. Mr. Not So Much, who had decided, as long as he was there, to stay for the program, took out his handkerchief, a great tremendous thing, and blew his nose.

11

Merry Christmas

Later that night, when the guests had gone home and all the little girls had gone to bed, Miss Plum and Miss Lavender got out the presents that were hidden in the closet. They put the presents into the twenty-eight stockings hung around the parlor. As many stockings as there was room for were hung by the fireplace; the rest were hung on doorknobs and chair backs. Into each stocking went an orange and an apple and a little box of candy and nuts; then in went a new box of crayons and a coloring book all rolled up like a tube so it would fit into the stocking. Then into some stockings went whistles, and into some stockings rubber balls, and into some stockings toy pipes for blowing bubbles. The clock on the mantel ticked on and on and on. Outside the snow had stopped falling. The streets and yards of Butterfield Square lay soft and white, gleaming in the light of streetlamps. Even the wind had sighed itself away to nothing.

The fire in the parlor burned lower and lower, and at last Miss Plum and Miss Lavender had filled every stocking. Then they went to the closet one more time and dragged out the big cardboard box of Christmas dolls.

"What will we do with *these* dolls?" Miss Plum said. She took Florabelle and Lily down from the piano and held them out at arm's length thoughtfully.

"Please give us to Tatty! Please give us to Tatty!" the dolls called. But of course Miss Lavender and Miss Plum could not hear them.

After a minute Miss Lavender said, "Tatty liked them so much. But I suppose it wouldn't be fair to give Tatty two extra dolls, would it?"

"No, I suppose not," Miss Plum said.

"But we could give her the rag doll for her Christmas doll," Miss Lavender said, "instead of one of those others. Tatty seemed to like the rag doll so much."

"And this other little doll would have been thrown away if Tatty hadn't fixed her up," Miss Plum said. "I don't think any of the other girls would mind if we let Tatty keep her, too—do you?"

"No, I'm sure the other girls wouldn't mind," Miss Lavender agreed eagerly.

She went over to the table and took the wrapping paper from the drawer. Florabelle and Lily were laid together side by side, and rolled up in soft white tissue paper. Then they were wrapped in bright red and green Christmas paper, and tied around with a good big piece of ribbon. They made a bulky package, and Miss Lavender and Miss Plum set it aside in a special place so they would be sure it was given to the right girl.

"Now we have an extra Christmas doll," Miss Lavender reminded Miss Plum. Again uncertainty settled over the two ladies. They looked at all the red and green packages lying in the cardboard box, and then Miss Plum snapped her fingers.

"We will give the extra doll to Cook's little granddaughter!"

"What a good idea," said Miss Lavender. "Won't Cook be pleased." She took one of the Christmas dolls and set it beside Cook's Christmas present, which was a box of pincushions and bookmarks and calendars made for Cook by the twenty-eight little girls.

"I'm so glad you thought of that," Miss Lavender said admiringly to Miss Plum. Miss Plum always seemed to know just the right thing to do.

Then they took out all the other wrapped Christmas dolls in the cardboard box and set them under the Christmas tree where the girls would find them Christmas morning.

When Miss Lavender and Miss Plum were finished at last it was very late. They went up to

their beds very tired and very happy. The parlor
was dark and silent, and outside the whole city
gleamed with fresh white snow . . . and then
slowly it began to grow light . . . and lighter
. . . and lighter . . . until it was Christmas
morning, and all the Christmas dolls could hear
the excited cries of little girls in the bedrooms
above, and the sound of their steps

running

down

the

stairs!

Into the parlor they burst, preceded only a second by Miss Plum and Miss Lavender, who turned on the Christmas tree lights. The little girls ran about finding their stockings, and then each little girl picked a package from under the tree.

"We have put your package here on the sofa,

Tatty," Miss Lavender whispered to Tatty, and led her aside to where Florabelle and Lily lay wrapped and tied with Christmas ribbon.

"My wish has come true!" Tatty exclaimed, as she tore away the paper and saw Florabelle and Lily.

"Our wish has come true, too," Lily and Florabelle said. They had so much to say to her—and they had all the time they needed to say it, for now they were going to belong to her, to their dear, dear Tatty. It was the most wonderful Christmas they had ever known.

"Don't eat all your candy before breakfast," Miss Plum reminded the girls. But she was not sure that anyone was listening to her. They were all so busy showing each other their dolls and examining all the things tucked into their Christmas stockings. Cook came in by and by and opened her package and said she had always wanted some pincushions and bookmarks and calendars, and then Miss Lavender and Miss Plum opened their packages and found that they, too, had their whole next year's supply of pincushions and bookmarks and calendars—and also some nice chocolate fudge that Cook had helped the girls to make as an extra surprise for Miss Lavender and Miss Plum.

Later that day, the girls lined up their Christmas dolls along the parlor window seat and went out to play in the snow. The dolls sat and talked among themselves, mostly of how glad they were to be unwrapped at last. Miss Lavender and Miss Plum brought in a tea tray and sat down to relax by the fire and eat some of their Christmas fudge. They had found some cake left over from the night before, and they were eating this, too. It was so good with their tea.

"If the director could see all this frosting," Miss Lavender said; but Miss Plum was too contented to worry.

The fire sputtered and a log shifted and sent bright flames shooting up for a moment. From outside could be heard the shouts of the girls playing in the snow.

Florabelle and Lily sat close together on the window seat. They felt very peaceful and happy and drowsy.

"I wonder what will happen to Tatty when she grows up," Lily said dreamily.

"She will probably have some little girls of her own someday," Florabelle said. "She will be a beautiful lady with earrings and high heels. She'll probably forget she ever was a little girl who could talk to dolls."

Lily rested her new black curls against the window frame and watched the flickering firelight. "You may be right," she said very softly. . . . "You may be right."

The Christmas tree was very beautiful, and the fire on the hearth burned warm and bright.

It was a lovely, lovely Christmas.

About the Author

CAROL BEACH YORK has written both stories for younger children and teen-age novels; among them are *Miss Know It All* (the first Butterfield Square Story), *The Doll in the Bakeshop, The Ghost of the Isherwoods,* and *Until We Fall in Love Again,* published by Franklin Watts, Inc. In this, the second of the Butterfield Square stories, she shows her unerring talent for knowing what a child will regard as a truly delightful story—just for him or her.

The author is married and lives in Harvey, Illinois. According to Mrs. York, her young daughter Diana is her most severe critic.

If you'd like to meet the people in *The Christmas Dolls* once again, don't miss the first Butterfield Square Story—

MISS KNOW IT ALL
by Carol Beach York
ILLUSTRATED BY VICTORIA DE LARREA

There she stood on the doorstep of Number 18 Butterfield Square—a small lady with a shiny black pocketbook. Her name was Miss Know It All, and she was the most extraordinary visitor that anyone had ever seen. She knew everything; everything in the world!

No matter what questions the twenty-eight little girls who lived at Number 18 asked, Miss Know It All knew the answers. Every one.

Then it was time for Tatty, one of the smallest girls, to ask a question. It was a strange question, but the answer was even more strange. Miss Know It All said three words that no one had ever heard her say before. And those three words brought a very big problem to Number 18 Butterfield Square.